I AM REA

Yeti SPaghetti

SAMANTHA HAY

ILLUSTRATED BY

MARK BEECH

KINGFISHER
NEW YORK

For Alice and Archie

 **KINGFISHER**
LONDON & NEW YORK

Text copyright © Samantha Hay 2009
Illustrations copyright © Mark Beech 2009

Published in the United States by Kingfisher,
175 Fifth Ave., New York, NY 10010
Kingfisher is an imprint of Macmillan Children's Books, London.
All rights reserved.

Distributed in the U.S. by Macmillan, 175 Fifth Ave., New York, NY 10010
Distributed in Canada by H.B. Fenn and Company Ltd., 34 Nixon Road, Bolton, Ontario L7E 1W2

Library of Congress Cataloging-in-Publication data has been applied for.

ISBN: 978-0-7534-6308-6

Kingfisher books are available for special promotions and premiums. For details contact:
Special Markets Department, Macmillan, 175 Fifth Avenue, New York, NY 10010.

For more information, please visit www.kingfisherpublications.com

First American Edition June 2010
Printed in China
10 9 8 7 6 5 4 3 2 1

Contents

Chapter One

Peter was putting the final cherry on
the giant Jell-O mold that he was
decorating, when he heard a growl . . .
"Tingling taste buds," he groaned. "The
Yetis are back again!"

A big, furry face was peering through the kitchen window.

"GRRRRRRRR!" growled the Yeti as it reached out a long, hairy hand . . .

"Hey!" yelled Peter. "STOP!"

But it was too late. The Yeti was gone. And so was half the Jell-O!

Peter sighed. That was the problem with living in the village of Scoffi: the Yetis. A big gang of them lived on the large, snowy mountain above the village, and every day they thundered down into the town and made a nuisance of themselves.

You see, Scoffi was
famous for food.
Everyone who lived
in the village was
crazy about cooking.
All day they diced
and sliced, and grilled and
chilled, creating the most delicious
dishes you've ever tasted.

The food was so
fabulous that people
came from far
and wide to
try it. And
so did the
Yetis.

They were everywhere: hanging around
houses and growling at windows . . .
trying to steal tidbits of whatever tasty
treats the villagers were making.

9

Peter shook his head.

It had to stop.

In two days' time it
would be the annual
Scoffi cooking
competition, and
chefs would be
entering from all
over the world.
Peter was hoping to
be the youngest-ever
winner. He was already the best cook
in Scoffi. But more than anything, he
wanted to win the competition and
prove to the world that Scoffi chefs
really were the best!

The only problem was the Yetis . . .

Chapter Two

The Mayor of Scoffi called a meeting.
Everyone came—including several
Yetis, who were sniffing around the
refreshments table.

"We have to get rid of them," said the
Mayor, pointing at the Yetis. "If we
can't, I'm canceling the competition!
I won't let Scoffi become the
laughingstock of the world," he said
angrily.

12

Peter sighed. His dreams of winning
the competition were sagging like
soggy sardine sandwiches.
But just then, a man in a dark cloak
appeared . . .

"I believe you have a Yeti problem,"
said the mysterious stranger.
Everyone nodded.
"Well, I might be able to help . . ."
The man whisked off his cloak to
reveal a bright green pair of shorts
and a tall hat with a huge red feather.

14

"I'm Yann the yodeler," he said

cheerfully.

The Mayor sighed. "That's all I need."
But before he could say another word,
Yann began . . .

"YODEL-AY-EEE-OOO!"

Peter made a face. It sounded awful.

The Yetis didn't like it, either.

They squealed and squirmed, growled and groaned,

and then ran away as fast as their big, furry legs would carry them.

It had worked. The Yetis were gone.

Chapter Three

It was competition day, and all the
villagers were up early, roasting and
toasting, chopping and wok-ing, all
hoping their own dish would catch the

eye of the head judge, Barry Baloney.
Peter was working hard, too,
decorating a huge pineapple cake.

Proudly, Peter carried his cake to the town hall, where the tables groaned under the weight of the goodies. There were fabulous flans. Wonderful waffles. Lovely lasagnas. Incredible ice creams.

And right in the middle of the table,
Peter placed his perfect pineapple cake.
But just then, there was a mighty
CRASH, and the doors of the town
hall were thrown open!

"Curdling custards!" gasped
Peter. "It's a Yeti!"
"GRRRRRRRRR!" the Yeti
growled.
Everyone watched in horror.
Everyone except Peter, who had
noticed something rather strange . . .

The Yeti

was carrying

a saucepan.

"ARRRGH!" screamed everyone . . .
except Peter.

Dishes were dropped, spoons were
scattered, and people dived under tables.
And then Yann appeared.
"YODEL-AY-EEE-OOO!"

"Hey! Stop yodeling!" shouted Peter,
whose nose had picked up the most
delicious smell coming from the
Yeti's saucepan.

But no one heard him over the noise.

"YODEL-AY-EEE-OOO!"

Peter raced over to the Yeti and peered
into the saucepan. It
looked like . . .
"Spaghetti?"
asked Peter.
The Yeti
nodded.
Peter's mouth watered.
The spaghetti glistened
like gold. The sauce
was the color
of rubies.
It was the most
amazing spaghetti
Peter had ever seen.
But there was no time to admire it.

"YODEL-AY-
EEE-OOO!"
The yodeling was
too much for the Yeti.
It clutched its saucepan to its
chest and ran out the door.

Chapter Four

Enough was enough.

Peter grabbed the closest thing, which just happened to be his own perfect pineapple cake, and flung it at Yann. That stopped him.

"BE QUIET, ALL OF YOU!" shouted
Peter.

Eventually, everyone was silent.

"That Yeti wasn't dangerous," said Peter.

"Hairy bears aren't welcome here!"
insisted the Mayor.

"But you don't understand," said Peter.
"I think he wants to enter our cooking
competition."

Everyone burst out laughing.

"Don't be silly!" exclaimed the Mayor.
"Yetis can't cook! Now, let's get on
with the judging."

And that was that.

Peter felt like crying.

Not only had the Yeti and his
spaghetti been sent away, but Peter's
perfect pineapple cake was ruined, too.

There was no point in staying.

With a heavy heart and a tear in
his eye, Peter left the town hall
and headed home.

Chapter Five

But Peter wasn't the only one crying.
Sitting outside the town hall, sniffling
into his saucepan, was the big, hairy Yeti.

Peter sat down next to him. And despite feeling sad, his tummy rumbled— the spaghetti smelled so good.

The Yeti stopped sniffling and held out his saucepan to Peter.

"You want me to try it?" asked Peter hopefully.

The Yeti nodded.

Peter dipped his finger into the sauce
and tasted it.
KAZOW!

His taste buds lit up
like twinkling lights.
"WOWZERS!" he
gasped. "It's delicious!"

And then suddenly, an idea popped into his head.

Peter picked up the saucepan and dashed back into the town hall, where the judging was almost over.

Carefully and quietly, so that nobody
spotted him, Peter placed the saucepan
at the end of the table.

A small man appeared with an
enormous spoon. It was the head
judge, Barry Baloney.

He dipped his spoon into the saucepan
and tasted the spaghetti.
A smile appeared on his face.
"It's good," he said.

He dipped his spoon again and tasted more. "It's *very* good," he said, smacking his lips together and grinning. "In fact, it's the best. Forget the rest. This spaghetti is the winner!"

Chapter Six

"Who created this masterpiece?"
boomed the Mayor.

Peter stepped forward. "That's Yeti
Spaghetti!" he said, pointing at the
saucepan. "And the chef who made
it is the poor Yeti you frightened
away earlier."

"Did someone say 'Yeti'?" asked Yann, appearing suddenly, still covered in Peter's pineapple cake.

"Yes, I did!" said Peter sternly. "But don't even think of yodeling—or you'll get a pan of spaghetti on your head, too."

Yann zipped his lips, while Barry Baloney
reached out and tasted some cake that
was clinging to the top of Yann's head.
"Mmmm," he mumbled, "delicious!"
And he reached for some more.
The Mayor folded his arms angrily.

"A Yeti cannot win this competition!"

"No, he can't," agreed Barry Baloney.

"Not on his own—because this cake is excellent, too. I've decided to have two winners: Yeti Spaghetti and this perfect pineapple cake."

Everyone was shocked. And stunned.
And a little annoyed.

But not for long. Soon the celebrations
began . . .
And the Yeti and Peter shared a big
gold trophy, which they carried proudly
around the village for all to see.

45

ALL the Yetis turned out to be terrific cooks, which was why they'd been hanging around Scoffi, bothering everyone—they were desperate to share recipes.

And Scoffi became even more famous—for its amazing Yeti chefs! The only person who wasn't pleased was Yann—because now that the Yetis were welcome in Scoffi, yodeling was definitely off the menu.

About the author and illustrator

Samantha Hay worked in TV before escaping to Scoffi to write children's books. She lives there with her husband, two children, and a giant African land snail named Snaily. "I love spaghetti," says Sam, "but unfortunately, I'm terrible at cooking. But now that we live in Scoffi, we enjoy great grub, cooked for us every day by the Yeti Spaghetti chef himself. Delicious!"

Mark Beech enjoys two things as much as he enjoys illustrating—yummy food and yodeling! So imagine his surprise when he discovered the town of Scoffi—truly a home away from home! Mark now lives in Scoffi and can often be found drawing in the town square while eating his favorite food, spaghetti Bolognese–flavored ice cream, made by his Yeti friends!

Strategies for Independent Readers

Predict

Think about the cover, illustrations, and the title
of the book. What do you think this book will be about?
While you are reading think about what may
happen next and why.

Monitor

As you read ask yourself if what you're reading makes sense.
If it doesn't, reread, look at the illustrations, or read ahead.

Question

Ask yourself questions about important ideas
in the story such as what the characters might
do or what you might learn.

Phonics

If there is a word that you do not know, look carefully
at the letters, sounds, and word parts that you do know.
Blend the sounds to read the word. Ask yourself if this is
a word you know. Does it make sense in the sentence?

Summarize

Think about the characters, the setting where the
story takes place, and the problem the characters faced
in the story. Tell the important ideas in the beginning,
middle, and end of the story.

Evaluate

Ask yourself questions like: Did you like the story?
Why or why not? How did the author make the story
come alive? How did the author make the story fun to
read? How well did you understand the story? Maybe
you can understand it better if you read it again!